AND THE TIGER

Dorla never imagines that Dilly is taking her seriously, when she tells him fantastic stories of sabre-tooth tigers eating little dinosaurs. And then one afternoon, Titan, a sabre-tooth tiger comes to visit . . .

TONY BRADMAN

DiLLY

AND THE TIGER

Illustrated by Susan Hellard

MAMMOTH

First published in 1988
by Piccadilly Press
Paperback edition published 1989 by Mammoth
an imprint of Reed International Books Limited
Michelin House, 81 Fulham Road, London SW3 6RB
and Auckland, Melbourne, Singapore and Toronto

Reprinted 1990, 1991, 1992 (twice), 1993, 1994 (three times), 1995

Text copyright © Tony Bradman 1988
Illustrations copyright © Susan Hellard 1988

ISBN 0 7497 0021 1

A CIP catalogue record for this title
is available from the British Library

Printed and bound in Great Britain
by Cox & Wyman Ltd, Reading, Berkshire

Contents

1.   DILLY AT THE TOYSHOP

One Saturday, we had to go to the Shopping Cavern. As soon as we arrived, Dilly started yelling and bouncing up and down.

"Dilly!" said Mother. "Will you please stop doing that! What do you think you are, a yo-yo?"

"But Mother," said Dilly. "Look! A toyshop!"

He was right. There *was* a toyshop, a brand new one. He ran up to it and

1

pressed his snout against the window.

"Can we go in, Mother?" he said.

"I suppose so," said Mother, with a sigh. "But we're not buying anything . . . Dilly, are you listening?"

Dilly had already run into the shop. As soon as he saw all the amazing toys inside, he stood absolutely still, his mouth open and his eyes as wide as swamp bubbles.

"*Wow*!" he said. There were so many toys, we didn't know where to start

2

looking.

"Come on, you two," Father said. "We haven't got all day."

I went over to a big display of dinosaur dolls with Father. The one I liked best was Dindy. You can buy lots of different clothes to dress her up in, and special ribbons for her tail. A Dindy doll costs quite a lot of money, but Father said that if I saved my pocket money, it wouldn't be too long before I could buy one.

After a while, Father said we'd better find the others. They were in another part of the shop, looking at a display of toy dino-cars, the sort you sit in and pedal. Dilly was sitting inside a beautiful green and yellow one.

"Come on, Dilly," said Father. "It's time to go."

"But I don't want to go, Father, I like

it here, broomm, broomm, beep beep!"
said Dilly. "And I want this toy
dino-car."

"Now, Dilly," said Father. "Mother
said we weren't going to buy any toys
today, and besides, a toy dino-car is very
expensive."

Dilly reached into the pocket of his
dungarees, dug down deep, and pulled
out something very small. It was a shiny
coin.

"It's all right, Father," he said with a
smile. "I've got some money."

"I'm afraid that's not enough, Dilly," said Father.

Dilly's smile vanished.

"Well, how much is enough?" he said. He looked quite cross and sulky.

"More than you can afford at the moment, I'm afraid," said Father. "Now come along . . . "

"But I want it," said Dilly, in a small, whiny voice.

"You could save up for it," I said. Dilly didn't understand, so I explained how I wasn't going to spend my pocket money when I got it every week. Instead, I was going to save it so that I

could buy a Dindy doll.

"That's a good idea, Dorla," said Father, who kept looking at his watch. "But can we talk about it later, *after* we've been to the supermarket?"

The next day, I asked Mother and Father if I could earn some extra pocket money by helping around the house. That way, I would be able to save up for my Dindy doll more quickly. Mother and Father said it was OK, so long as I really did help.

Dilly asked if he could do the same.

"I'm going to save up and buy the toy dino-car," he said.

"That might take too long, Dilly," said Mother. "A toy dino-car is very expensive."

"I don't mind how long it takes, Mother," said Dilly.

"Well, we'll see . . . " said Mother. I

didn't think he would help. But he did. Usually he won't get himself ready in the morning, but every day that week he got up and washed and dressed himself, without being told to. He kept his room

tidy, helped to set the table and clear it after meals, and watered the fern plants in the garden.

At the end of the week, Mother and Father said they were very pleased with what we'd done, and gave us both our extra pocket money.

7

We did the same the next week, and the week after that Mother gave Dilly a jar to save his money in, and soon he had quite a few shiny coins. Almost every day, he asked her to count it for him. Some days he even asked her to weigh it on the kitchen scales.

"Have I got enough yet for the toy dino-car, Mother?" he said one day.

"That dino-car costs a lot, Dilly," she said. Just at that moment there was a knock on the door.

"But how much have I got?" said Dilly.

"What, Dilly?" said Mother, as she

went to the door. It was the post dinosaur. "I can't remember now," she said. "Quite a lot, anyway."

Dilly didn't say anything. He just smiled.

The next day was shopping day again, and we went to the Shopping Cavern as usual. Dilly insisted on bringing his jar of money with him, and when we arrived at the toyshop, he ran straight in.

"Dilly! Come back this instant!" called Father, and we all ran in after him.

It didn't take long to find Dilly. He was sitting in the beautiful green and yellow toy dino-car, making lots of noise and crashing it into the other ones on display.

"Dilly!" said Father, in a very cross voice. "This isn't a racing track! Stop that immediately!"

"It's OK, Father," said Dilly, with a great big smile, "it's going to be my dino-car now. I've saved up my money, so I can buy it today."

"I'm sorry, Dilly," said Father, "but I don't think you can."

Dilly looked confused.

"But Mother said the dino-car costs a lot," said Dilly. "And she said I had a lot of money, too."

"But you still haven't got enough, Dilly," said Mother. "Look . . . I'll count it for you. Then you'll see."

Mother took Dilly's money jar over to the cash desk. She emptied it, and the nice dinosaur who serves you helped her to count it. There wasn't enough to buy the toy dino-car.

"I'm sorry, Dilly," said Mother. "You *have* got enough to buy something less expensive, though."

"But I want the toy dino-car," said Dilly, in a very cross voice. "And I don't want anything else." He sat there, arms folded, looking very sulky.

The dinosaur from behind the cash desk came over.

"You can always sit in the dino-car when you come to the toy shop," she said with a smile. "And in the meantime you can keep saving."

Dilly didn't say anything. He just stuck his tongue out at her.

"Dilly!" said Father, in a very cross voice. "Don't be so rude! If you're not out of there by the time I count to three,

you're going to be in big trouble. One
. . . two . . . "

Father never got to number three.
Dilly opened his mouth . . . and let rip
with a 150-mile-per-hour, ultra-special
super-scream, the kind that sends us

diving for cover and makes everyone
else run out of the shop.

His bad behaviour didn't end there,
either. Even when he'd stopped
screaming, he wouldn't get out of the toy
dino-car. He held on to it as tight as he

could, and kicked and swished his tail around. Father had to prise his paws off, and as he was struggling to carry him out of the shop, they bumped into a big display of building boulders and knocked it right over.

Of course, Mother and Father were very, very cross with Dilly. They told him off, and as soon as we got home, they sent him straight to his room without any supper.

Later, after Dilly said he was sorry, Mother and Father had a talk with him. They said it took far too long to save up for big things like the dino-car. It was the sort of toy you got for Christmas, or your birthday – but only if you were a good little dinosaur.

Dilly looked thoughtful for a moment.

"If I'm *really* good," he said, "could we have Christmas or my birthday early?"

Mother and Father laughed.

2.   DILLY AND THE TIGER

One day Dilly and I were watching a programme about mammoths on TV. As soon as it was over, Dilly jumped up and started pretending to be one.

"Hey, look out!" I said.

It was too late. Dilly crashed into the little table where Mother puts our drinks. The cups went flying, and there was pineapple juice all over the rug.

Mother heard the noise and came in.

"Dilly!" she said. "You're like a

sabre-tooth tiger in a china shop."

Dilly said he was sorry. Mother mopped up the mess while we picked up the cups and straightened the table.

"Mother," said Dilly when everything was tidy, "what's a sabre-tooth tiger?"

"Well, Dilly," said Mother, "it's a large, fierce creature with two very big teeth . . . I think we might have a picture of one in a book, somewhere . . . "

Mother found the book, and showed it to Dilly. It explained how sabre-tooth tigers hunted all sorts of animals, even mammoths. Dilly sat quietly listening.

"Mother," he said, after a while, "do sabre-tooth tigers eat . . . dinosaurs?"

"No, Dilly," she laughed. "In fact, quite a few dinosaurs have them as pets."

Dilly seemed quite impressed. The next day, he got Mother to make him some big teeth out of paper so that he could pretend to be a sabre-tooth.

"You're a big, woolly mammoth," he growled at me later from the back of an armchair, "and I'm going to . . . EAT YOU UP!"

He jumped with a roar, but I got out of the way . . . and he landed right on top of the little table again. There was a great crash. Our cups were broken, and so was the table.

Mother was really angry. She didn't believe it was just Dilly's fault, so she told us both off and sent us to our rooms.

I was cross, because that meant I had to miss a programme I really like, *Dinosaur Street*. So as we were going upstairs, I said I hoped a sabre-tooth tiger would come to our house soon and gobble Dilly up, tail and all.

"But Mother said they don't eat dinosaurs," said Dilly, sticking his tongue out.

"She only said that because she didn't want to frighten you," I said. "They do really, and their favourite meal is a juicy little dinosaur, just like you!"

on toast?
...lightly boiled?
...roasted?

Dilly didn't say anything. He went into his room, and I didn't think any more about it.

Later, we both came downstairs and

said we were sorry. Mother was telling us we weren't ever to be so naughty again, when the dino-phone rang.

"Hello?" said Mother. "Oh yes . . . of course . . . how wonderful! . . . Bye!"

She put the dino-phone down.

"Well, Dilly," she said with a smile, "that was Dixie's mother. She's bringing Dixie over tomorrow."

Dilly started bouncing up and down with excitement. Dixie is his best friend, and there's nothing he likes better than playing with her.

"Oh yes, I nearly forgot," said Mother. "Dixie will have a surprise for you tomorrow, too."

"What sort of surprise, Mother?" said Dilly.

"Ah, it won't be a surprise if I tell you, will it?" said Mother with a smile. "You'll find out tomorrow."

The next day, Dilly couldn't wait for Dixie to arrive. At last we heard footsteps coming up the path, and a knock on the door. There were some other strange noises, too – a sort of growling. Dilly didn't seem to notice anything, though.

Mother opened the door, and Dilly rushed forward.

"Hi, Dixie, where's the sur . . . " he started to say, but then he stopped. He stood there, with his mouth open, looking at what we could all see on the doorstep.

A great big, furry, stripy, growling . . . sabre-tooth tiger.

Standing next to it was Dixie. She was holding a lead which was attached to the tiger's collar, and she had a huge smile on her face.

"Surprise!" she said. "Do you like my

tiger, Dilly? His name's Titan."

Dilly didn't say anything.

Dixie told us all about her new pet.
She said that even though he looked
very big, he was still only a cub, and that
he would get much bigger and stronger.

"Why don't you take him out into the
garden, Dixie?" said Mother. "You'll
enjoy that, won't you, Dilly? Dilly!
Where are you?"

Dilly had gone upstairs. He said he
didn't want to go in the garden, either.
Mother said she thought he was
probably a little jealous of Titan, and
asked me to play with Dixie instead.

21

It was fun playing with Titan, but very tiring. At last he lay down for a sleep. Mother asked me to try and get Dilly to come out of his room, so I went indoors. I knocked on his door.

"Come on, Dilly," I said. "You can't sit in there all day."

There was no answer.

"Dixie will probably have to go home soon," I said. "I've been playing with Titan, and he's gone to sleep."

There was still no answer.

"Suit yourself," I said, and went downstairs.

A few minutes later, Dilly came down too. He acted very strangely, though. He kept looking through all the doors and over his shoulder.

"Oh, hello, Dilly," said Mother when she saw him. "We were just going to have a drink and a snack. Would you like something?"

"Er . . . what?" said Dilly, looking round, quickly. "Oh, yes please."

Mother gave him a packet of crispy fern stalks and a cup of pineapple juice.

"We're all having ours in the garden," she said. "Are you coming out too? It's a lovely day."

"Er . . . no, Mother," he said.

So Dilly stayed inside. We sat under the giant fern in the garden, near Titan.

After a while, he yawned, stretched, and stood up. He trotted round the garden for a while, and then he went indoors.

"I wonder why Dilly's acting so strangely . . . " Mother began to say, when all of a sudden, there was the sound of . . . an ultra-special, 150-mile-per-hour super-scream, the sort that makes us all run into the house to see what's wrong.

We found Dilly standing in a corner. He had both his eyes shut tight, and looked terrified.

Titan was standing in front of Dilly. As we watched, his big red tongue came out and licked Dilly's snout with a loud, rasping noise . . . slurrrppp!

"What on earth is the matter, Dilly?" said Mother.

"Titan . . . tried . . . to . . . eat me!" he said, and burst into tears.

"There, there, Dilly," she said. "He was only trying to be friendly. Anyway, don't you remember what I said? Tigers don't eat dinosaurs."

"But Dorla told me they did," sniffed Dilly.

"Oh, did she now?" said Mother. "Dorla . . . where do you think you're going? I want to have a word with you . . ."

Of course, Mother was very cross with me. She said it wasn't very nice to try and frighten someone, whether they'd made you miss your favourite TV programme or not. I said I was sorry, and that I wouldn't do it ever again.

It took ages to calm Dilly down, and even when he was quiet, he still didn't want to go near Titan. It was Dixie who made everything all right in the end, though. She told Dilly Titan was sorry

25

he had upset him, and that he wanted to be his friend.

Titan was lying down in front of Dilly, his head on his paws, and he did seem to be saying he was sorry. Dilly gave him a very careful look . . . and then he patted his head once, very quickly.

But by the time Dixie went home, Dilly was very friendly with Titan. In fact, they were so friendly that Dilly was having rides on Titan's back, and didn't want him to go.

At bedtime that evening, Dilly charged around pretending to be a tiger. And then I heard him ask Mother if we could have a tiger, just like Titan.

"I don't know about that, Dilly," I heard her say. "I think one tiger in the family is quite enough!"

3. DILLY AND THE CONTRARY DAY

"Mother," said Dilly at breakfast yesterday, "will you play with me today?"

Now if there's one thing Dilly really enjoys, it's having Mother or Father play with him. But they don't often have the time.

"I'm afraid not, Dilly," said Mother.

"But why?" said Dilly.

"I've got too much to do," said Mother. "Your father and I are having some friends round for dinner this evening, so we're going to be very busy."

"But it's not fair," said Dilly. "You never play with me."

"I'm sorry, Dilly," said Mother, "but today I just can't. Besides, I was hoping that you and Dorla would help me. Wouldn't you like to?"

"No I would not!" shouted Dilly. Then he got down from the table and stomped away, STAMP! STAMP! STAMP!

Mother was a little cross with Dilly, and told him off. She also said he had to put the toys back in our big toy cupboard. The night before he had got most of them out, and then left them on the floor at bedtime.

Dilly didn't say anything. But I could tell he wasn't very happy.

28

Mother started tidying up the downstairs rooms. She got the vacuum cleaner out, but it didn't seem to be working properly.

"The fern pod probably needs changing," said Mother. "There's a new one in the store cupboard, Dorla. Run along and fetch it for me, will you?"

The store cupboard is in the same room as the big toy cupboard, along with a few other cupboards and boxes where we keep all sorts of things.

When I got there, I pushed the door, but it wouldn't open. I pushed again, harder, and it opened a tiny crack.

I peeked through . . . and I could hardly believe what I saw.

"What's taking so long?"

It was Mother. I told her I couldn't open the door, and she began to look worried.

"Is Dilly in there?" she said.

"Er . . . yes, Mother," I said, "but I think . . ."

Mother didn't listen. She just pushed the door as hard as she could. There was a crunching, cracking sound, and the door moved back slowly, until it was half open.

And there before us was the biggest mess you've ever seen.

Dilly hadn't tidied his toys away. Instead, he'd got them all out and piled them in a great heap. Then he must have emptied the other cupboards and boxes, too, and put everything from them on top of the mound of toys. It was the mound that had been blocking the door.

"Dilly!" said Mother, in a shocked voice, "what have you got to say for yourself?"

Dilly didn't say anything. He just stuck his tongue out.

Of course, Mother was very, very cross. She was even more cross when she found out that the crunching, cracking sound had been the spare fern pod for the vacuum cleaner breaking when she opened the door.

It was the only one we had, too.

"I'll never get everything done today!" she said. She told Dilly off

31

again, and sent him straight to his room.

It took ages to clear up the mess he had made. After we'd done it, Mother looked at her watch.

"Oh my," she said, "if I don't get those swamp moss rolls in the oven soon they won't be ready in time!"

Later, at lunchtime, Mother said Dilly could come out of his room if he was sorry and promised to behave. He said he would, but I didn't think he really meant it.

I was right, too. Things went from bad to worse. In the afternoon, Mother said she was going to do the upstairs rooms while Father started preparing the rest of the dinner.

"So you two can go outside and play in the garden," she said. "I don't want you under my feet while I'm busy."

But Dilly, of course, had other ideas.

"Can you play with me now, Mother?" he said.

"I've already told you once I can't, Dilly," she said. "Now be a good little dinosaur and do what you're told for once."

"I won't!" said Dilly. "I don't want to play in the smelly old garden," he said, looking really sulky.

Mother looked even more cross than ever.

"Dilly, why are you being so contrary today?" she said. "I think if you say 'No' or 'I don't want to' again today, I'll scream."

Dilly opened his mouth to say something. For a second, I thought he was going to do what he usually does when he can't get his own way . . . but he didn't. He closed his mouth again, and we both went outside to play.

33

I didn't stay outside for long, though. Dilly was in a very bad mood, and kept saying horrible things. So I decided to go indoors.

"Just make sure you wipe your feet before you come in, Dorla," Father said. "The garden's a little muddy, and we don't want the floors to get all dirty after we've just cleaned them."

I wiped my feet carefully, and went upstairs. Mother had finished tidying, and said that she was going to start getting herself ready.

"I've bought a new dress to wear this evening," she said. "What do you think of it, Dorla?"

Mother got the new dress out of her wardrobe to show me. It was a beautiful swamp green, with yellow stripes. I said it was lovely.

"I'm going to have a bath now,"

Mother said. "You could go and help
your father with the cooking, Dorla. Tell
him those swamp moss rolls have got to
come out of the oven at six o'clock, or
they'll be spoilt."

I said I would.

Mother went into the bathroom, and I
went downstairs to help Father. It didn't
take long to finish everything, and then
there wasn't much else to do. So Father

decided to have a shower, and I went to my room.

We had both forgotten about Dilly.

About half an hour later, I heard them come out of the bathroom.

"Oh, no!" I heard Mother say. I went to see what was the matter.

Mother and Father were on the landing, looking down at the carpet. There were small, muddy footprints all over it. They came up the stairs and went in the direction of Mother and Father's bedroom.

"Dilly . . . " Mother said, and opened her bedroom door.

The bedroom was in a terrible mess. Someone had been drawing pictures with Mother's make-up on the dressing table mirror. A lot of the drawers were open, with everything hanging out of them. There were muddy footprints

everywhere, too, even on the bed.

And that's where Dilly was standing.
In fact, he was bouncing up and down on
Mother's new dress, which was under his
feet, all screwed up and covered in mud.

Mother was *furious*.

"Dilly Dinosaur," she said from
between clenched teeth, "get off that
bed *immediately*!"

"No! I will not," he said, and stuck his
tongue out at her. She was about to say

something when she started to sniff.

"What's that smell?" she said.

"Oh no!" said Father, rushing out. "The swamp moss rolls! They're burning!"

Mother had a very strange look on her face. She shut her eyes, opened her mouth . . . and out came something that sounded just like one of Dilly's ultra-special, 150-mile-per-hour super-screams.

Dilly and I dived for cover, and we didn't come out until Mother had stopped.

Dilly was in a lot of trouble. Father was so cross he actually spanked him, and that's something he hardly ever does. He was also sent to bed without any supper.

The next day, Mother and Father said their evening hadn't turned out too badly in the end. Dilly looked very ashamed, and said he was sorry.

For the rest of that day, he kept giving Mother funny looks.

"Mother," I heard him say at last, "you've got a very loud scream."

"Now you know where you get it from," she said, and winked.

Dilly just smiled.

4. DILLY AND THE BIRTHDAY TREAT

Last week, Dilly asked Father if it was his birthday soon.

"It's not too far away now, Dilly," said Father. "About a month or so."

"Yippee!" shouted Dilly. "And can I have a birthday treat this year, like Dorla did for *her* birthday?"

For my birthday this year, instead of giving me an ordinary party, Mother and Father had taken me on an outing with some of my friends from school. We went swamp wallowing, and we had a wonderful time.

"I don't know," said Father. "You're still a little young for an outing like that."

"It's not fair," said Dilly. "I want to go swamp wallowing with my friends, just like Dorla did."

"I suppose it might be all right," said Father. "You *have* been doing very well in your swamp wallowing lessons."

"Yes, I have," said Dilly, with a big smile. "I can almost wallow a whole width now."

"But we'll only be able to take a few of your friends," said Father.

"That's OK, Father," said Dilly. "We could take Dixie, and Doopa, and a couple of others."

"Well . . . that should be OK, Dilly," said Father. "I'll get everything arranged."

41

"And can we go to MacDinosaur's for lunch that day, too?" said Dilly.

"I suppose so," said Father, with a sigh.

Later, Mother and Father asked me if I would go along. They said they would need my help to look after Dilly and his little friends. I said I would.

From then on, Dilly spent most of his time thinking about his outing.

"What time will my friends arrive on my birthday, Father?" he would ask.

"What, Dilly? I think we've asked them to come at about twelve on the invitation."

"And will we go straight to MacDinosaur's?"

"I should think so, Dilly," Father would sigh.

"Good," Dilly would say. "Now I'll sit between Dixie and Derri, and I'll have a

Triple-Dipple Bronto-burger and an extra thick milk shake . . . "

Dilly wanted to plan what his friends would have for lunch, what games they would play in the dino-car on the way to the swamp, who would get in the swamp first (that was him), and who would get out last (that was him, too). And he kept repeating "It's going to be the BEST BIRTHDAY EVER."

Finally, it was the morning of Dilly's birthday. And didn't we know it!

I was woken up very, very early by the noise coming from Dilly's room. It sounded as if he was pulling things out of his drawers. Then I heard him go into Mother and Father's room, so I went in too.

Dilly was dressed in his swamp wallowing outfit. He even had his mud wings on, although they weren't blown

up, and the mask and goggles Mother
and Father had bought him for doing so
well in his lessons.

"Yippee!" he shouted, and jumped on
the bed. Mother and Father were
snuggled deep down under the
bedclothes. I heard Father groan.

"Dilly," he said, "have you any idea
what time it is?"

"Yes, Father," Dilly laughed. "IT'S
BIRTHDAY TIME! AND IT'S GOING
TO BE THE BEST BIRTHDAY
EVER!"

And then he started to bounce up and down on the bed. As you can probably tell, Dilly was rather excited.

Dilly's present from Mother and Father was a Superdinosaur costume, and he was really pleased with it. I gave him a packet of candied fern flakes, and a card I'd made. Mother said that Grandma and Grandpa would come later with their present, after we got back from the outing. Dilly said he couldn't wait.

"Come on, Dilly," said Father when he got up to make breakfast. "Get your clothes on. You can't go around in your wallowing outfit all morning."

"But I don't want to get dressed, Father," said Dilly. "I want to go on my outing *now*."

"It isn't time to go yet," said Father. "Your friends won't be here until twelve, and it's only eight o'clock."

I could see Dilly wasn't very happy about that.

"Why don't you put your Superdinosaur costume on?" said Father, quickly. "I'm sure Dorla will help you . . . *won't* you, Dorla?"

"I suppose so," I said. "Come on, Dilly . . ."

After breakfast, Father said he was relying on me to help keep Dilly calm. He said that Dilly was already over-excited, and that if he got any worse, there was bound to be trouble. I said I would do my best.

The morning dragged by for all of us. Dilly soon got bored with playing at being Superdinosaur. And after that he was a real pest. He kept asking what time it was and whether his friends would arrive soon.

At last it was twelve o'clock, and there was a knock on the door. Dilly raced to the door shouting, "IT'S THE BEST BIRTHDAY EVER!" It was Doopa, and Dilly's other friends came soon after.

"Can we go now, Father?" said Dilly. He started to bounce up and down. "Can we go? Please? *Please*?"

We left the dino-car in the parking cave, and set off towards MacDinosaur's. But when we got there it looked very strange. The lights weren't on, and there were no people inside. Mother tried the doors, but they wouldn't open. There was a little sign on them. Father leant forward to read it.

"Closed . . . for . . . re-decoration," he read out, slowly. "Oh dear," he said, in an embarrassed voice. "I'm sorry, Dilly, but it looks as if we won't be able to have lunch at MacDinosaur's after all."

Dilly looked really disappointed. He loves going to MacDinosaur's. His snout started to wobble the way it always does when he's going to cry.

"But it's my birthday," he said, quietly.

"Never mind, Dilly," said Father with a smile. "We can have something to eat in the cafeteria at the swamp. You'd like that, wouldn't you?"

Dilly cheered up straight away.

'What did you say today was going to be?" asked Father.

"It's going to be THE BEST BIRTHDAY EVER!" shouted Dilly.

So we all piled back into the dino-car and went off to the swamp.

But when we got there, we found that it was very crowded. We had to park the dino-car a long way away, and it took ages to get into the cafeteria. And then there was a huge queue to get into the swamp itself.

It was absolutely packed. There was hardly room to do any wallowing at all,

and Dilly's friends didn't like all the
noise, and the big dinosaurs jumping in.
Father tried to make sure Dilly had a
good time, but it was impossible. Then,
just fifteen minutes or so after we'd got
in, the attendant said it was time to get
out.

"That's it, I'm afraid, Dilly," said
Father. "We have to go home now."

"But it's my birthday!" said Dilly,
with a sob . . . and then he let rip with
an ultra-special, 150-mile-per-hour
super-scream, the sort that empties the
swamp in seconds.

But it didn't make any difference. We still had to get out.

Poor Dilly cried all the way home, and he still didn't look very happy, even when Father brought out his cake and

we sang Happy Birthday to him.

A few minutes later, there was a knock on the door. It was Grandma and Grandpa . . . and they had brought Dilly an *enormous* present.

"Well, Dilly," said Grandpa. "What do you think this is?"

Everyone stopped stuffing themselves with cake and looked. Dilly didn't say anything. He just ripped off the paper as quickly as he could. And there before him was . . . the beautiful green and yellow toy dino-car he had seen in the toyshop ages ago. And then he smiled for the first time since we'd stood outside MacDinosaur's.

"So are you having a good birthday, Dilly?" Grandpa asked him.

Dilly thought for a while, and then looked at his new toy.

"I am now, Grandpa," he said, with a smile. "IT'S THE BEST BIRTHDAY EVER!"

Tony Bradman

DILLY AND THE GHOST

After Dilly persuades Father to read him ghost stories at bedtime, he's positive the house is haunted. But no-one in the family believes him. So Dilly decides to convince everyone that there really are ghosts about the house . . .

This is the seventh collection of stories about Dilly, the world's naughtiest dinosaur.

Tony Bradman

DILLY GOES ON HOLIDAY

Dilly and his family are off on holiday to the Swamp Land theme park. Dilly is sure he's going to have fun – but isn't too pleased when he finds that he's going to have to join the Tiny Tails. Then Dilly meets Dee who looks after the Tiny Tails – and decides that he's going to have a good holiday after all!

In this tenth book about Dilly the Dinosaur, Dilly also takes part in a Sports Day, puts on a magic show and finds a pet.

MEET THE WORLD'S NAUGHTIEST DINOSAUR!

Even though, as everyone knows, he's the world's naughtiest dinosaur Dilly still has lots of fans. Now that he is so famous he's started making special visits to bookshops to meet the people who enjoy reading about him. You might be able to meet him in your local book-shop – he usually tries to behave himself!

You can write to this address for more informa-tion about Dilly and his books and about other books published by MAMMOTH.

MAMMOTH Press Office,
38 Hans Crescent,
London SW1X 0LZ

A selected list of titles available from Mammoth

While every effort is made to keep prices low, it is sometimes necessary to increase prices at short notice. Mandarin Paperbacks reserves the right to show new retail prices on covers which may differ from those previously advertised in the text or elsewhere.

The prices shown below were correct at the time of going to press.

☐	7497 0366 0	**Dilly the Dinosaur**	Tony Bradman	£2.50
☐	7497 0137 4	**Flat Stanley**	Jeff Brown	£2.50
☐	7497 0306 7	**The Chocolate Touch**	P Skene Catling	£2.50
☐	7497 0568 X	**Dorrie and the Goblin**	Patricia Coombs	£2.50
☐	7497 0114 5	**Dear Grumble**	W J Corbett	£2.50
☐	7497 0054 8	**My Naughty Little Sister**	Dorothy Edwards	£2.50
☐	7497 0723 2	**The Little Prince (colour ed.)**	A Saint-Exupery	£3.99
☐	7497 0305 9	**Bill's New Frock**	Anne Fine	£2.99
☐	7497 0590 6	**Wild Robert**	Diana Wynne Jones	£2.50
☐	7497 0661 9	**The Six Bullerby Children**	Astrid Lindgren	£2.50
☐	7497 0319 9	**Dr Monsoon Taggert's Amazing Finishing Academy**	Andrew Matthews	£2.50
☐	7497 0420 9	**I Don't Want To!**	Bel Mooney	£2.50
☐	7497 0833 6	**Melanie and the Night Animal**	Gillian Rubinstein	£2.50
☐	7497 0264 8	**Akimbo and the Elephants**	A McCall Smith	£2.50
☐	7497 0048 3	**Friends and Brothers**	Dick King-Smith	£2.50
☐	7497 0795 X	**Owl Who Was Afraid of the Dark**	Jill Tomlinson	£2.99

All these books are available at your bookshop or newsagent, or can be ordered direct from the publisher. Just tick the titles you want and fill in the form below.

Mandarin Paperbacks, Cash Sales Department, PO Box 11, Falmouth, Cornwall TR10 9EN.

Please send cheque or postal order, no currency, for purchase price quoted and allow the following for postage and packing:

UK including BFPO £1.00 for the first book, 50p for the second and 30p for each additional book ordered to a maximum charge of £3.00.

Overseas including Eire £2 for the first book, £1.00 for the second and 50p for each additional book thereafter.

NAME (Block letters) ....

ADDRESS ....

....

☐ I enclose my remittance for ....

☐ I wish to pay by Access/Visa Card Number

Expiry Date